BETHANY'S SUBMISSION

DOMESTIC DISCIPLINE SPANKING ROMANCE

SUBMISSIVE WIVES
BOOK ONE

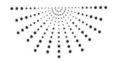

LEE RILEY

ABOUT THIS BOOK

Bethany and her husband Richard have been living a **Domestic Discipline** lifestyle for several years, but Bethany has never been able to fully submit to Richard's authority as **Head of Household**.

As a consequence, she is spanked and punished constantly. Richard loves his wife and wants to improve their marriage. He finds out about a Domestic Discipline Boot Camp, and although they can't attend, he implements a **submission training program** of his own.

Bethany readily consents, but is surprised when her husband asks for help from a stranger on her first day of training. She overcomes her resistance to her husband Richard's authority. Allowing herself to become his utter **slave** in every way, she is freed from her inhibitions and submits completely.

Bethany is required to do **whatever** her husband, Richard, orders as part of her **Domestic Discipline Boot Camp** style **submission training** and she learns to obey without question.

And when Bethany's **Domestic Discipline Boot Camp** is coming to an end and she followed her husband's orders to the letter, she finds herself bound and blindfolded, waiting in their hotel room for her final test...

Formerly published as "Riley Connors"

BETHANY'S SUBMISSION - PART 1

A DOMESTIC DISCIPLINE SPANKING ROMANCE

CHAPTER ONE

"Something has to change, Bethany," my husband told me in a tired voice.

Other than the thin cashmere sweater that I had worn to the ladies luncheon that afternoon, I was naked from the waist down. Draped over Richard's lap, my still firm ass cherry red and sore from yet another wooden paddle spanking, I could only nod through my tears.

We had been living a Domestic Discipline lifestyle for several years, and at first I had blamed my troubles with submission on being a beginner to DD. I had constantly forgotten my place, made silly mistakes, broken Richard's rules, and seemed to walk around with a bruised, aching bottom every day of the week.

But I wasn't a beginner anymore.

As my friend Sophie liked to say, Domestic Discipline was like a gym membership. It's not a question of whether *it* works, it's a question of whether you work at it.

"I've heard of something that might help us," Richard went on as he started to massage the pain away. "It's a Boot Camp for-- well, it's intended for those new to the DD lifestyle. I know we're not new, but-- it's designed as a training program for wives to learn complete submission to their Head of Household."

I perked up. I was very good at following programs. I started to roll off his lap so I could sit up and talk about it face to face. I got a stinging slap to my fiery bum for moving without permission, and settled back down distractedly.

"That's what I'm talking about, BeeBee--" Richard started to say at the same time that I asked a question.

"Where is the Boot Camp? When can we--"

Smack!

Would I ever learn? I sighed and settled down quietly on his lap, reminding myself that he would give me information as needed.

"The problem," Richard continued. "Is that I've got to fly out to the Cummington Group annual board meeting the same week that the upcoming Boot Camp session starts. And the next available session isn't until summer."

Finally pulling me off his lap, he positioned me on my knees in front of him. I saw a gleam of hope in his eyes, and smiled up at him. He leaned forward and kissed my forehead tenderly.

"I want you to come with me to the board meeting, Bee," he told me, more animated than I'd seen him in weeks. "I've downloaded the training guidelines from the Boot Camp's website, and I thought we could use the trip to do a mini-submission training camp of our own.

The official Boot Camp program is two full weeks, but it's designed for beginners. We've been doing this long enough that I'm hoping we can make some real progress in the few days we'll be gone."

I nodded and smiled. I loved the idea. I knew it would be a challenge, but I also believed in training, practice, and repetition. It's how I'd become a professional ballerina years ago, how I'd learned French in my 20's, and now - I hoped - how I would finally learn to be the truly submissive wife that my husband deserved.

"We've got to get to bed," he smiled down at me after glancing at his watch. "Let's finish up. I've got an 8:00 am meeting tomorrow."

"Yes, sir," I replied with an answering smile. "Thank you for the paddling." And then I unzipped him and pulled out his cock, so I could give him the formal thank you he deserved.

CHAPTER TWO

I had two days to rearrange my busy charity volunteer schedule, reschedule my personal appointments, arrange for household staff to manage things in my absence, and finish packing and making travel arrangements for Richard and me.

I was so focused on the whirlwind of activities that I have to admit I neglected my husband in little ways, and therefore continued to walk around stiffly from my frequently spanked bottom. The night before we were scheduled to fly out, he sat me down to go over our training program.

"Bethany," he addressed me formally. "To make the submission training work, we both need to agree on your unquestioning obedience during our trip. If you're able to spend this time *truly* submitting to my authority in every way, then when we return to our normal house rules your submission should be an ingrained habit. Which means your sweet little ass won't be sore quite as often."

I smiled wryly, trying not to squirm as I sat on that throbbing ass.

"I need your unconditional consent, BeeBee," he smiled down at me lovingly. "Because once we begin, there will be no backing out until the training period is over."

"I *do*, honey," I didn't have to think it over. I wanted this. "You know it's been such a struggle for me. I'm so grateful you've taken the time to put this together. Just tell me what I need to do and I promise, you'll have 100% obedience."

He smiled and told me the rules. Starting the next morning, he would address me by my full name to indicate when he was giving an order, and I was to refer to him only as "Sir" to help me remember to submit to his authority. I was to receive maintenance spankings morning and night. I was to formally thank him for every punishment with a blow job once the punishment was complete. And I was to obey him, without question, in all matters, during the training period.

"How long will the training last?" I asked, then added a cheeky "Sir" that made him smile down at me.

"Until we get home from the trip."

CHAPTER THREE

Startled out of a sound sleep, I blinked in confusion as the darkness was suddenly chased away by the bright bedside lamp.

"Bethany, get up," Richard ordered.

Groggy, I squinted at the digital clock next to the bed. It was 3:00 am. Rolling over sleepily I put a pillow over my head and mumbled something to my husband about our flight not being until 10 o'clock.

With a cold rush, the covers were whipped off me and my short nightgown yanked up. *Smack!* His bare hand came down on my exposed ass. I yelped and tried to jump up, but Richard wasn't having it. I got 20 stinging swats that had tears leaking out of my eyes before he let me up.

"Get up, Bethany," he repeated quietly.

Scrambling out of bed, I looked at him in confusion. Without thinking I reached a hand back to rub my sore bottom, but stopped mid-motion at his stern look.

"Bethany, when I give you an order, you will obey without question. When I punish you, you will thank me. If you want to do something that hasn't come from me--" he said with a pointed look at my frozen hand. "--you will ask my permission first. Your training period has begun. This is the last time I'll remind you. Is that clear?"

I gulped, then nodded. I was now fully awake, but the whole thing still felt surreal. Even though Richard had punished me before in his role as HOH, I had always back talked, argued, and questioned as I saw fit. Part of the reason our DD lifestyle had felt so difficult was this failure of mine to submit.

It was exactly the reason I *needed* this training.

Richard needed it too, I suddenly realized. My constant small rebellions against his authority had diluted his power to guide our lives the way he needed to. But now... my agreement to be totally submissive gave him permission to finally, fully take charge.

I felt my pussy tingle as what we were doing really hit me. My training meant I truly *couldn't* say no. And I felt... owned. Loved. Protected and safe in a way that I could never remember feeling before.

Without any hesitation, I let my natural impulse take over and fell to my knees in front of him.

"Thank you, sir," I whispered humbly. Pulling the waistband of his pajama bottoms down, I lovingly sucked his hardening cock into my mouth, reveling in my ability to give him this, in appreciation of all he was doing for me.

Running his hands through my sleep tangled hair, he let me suck him slow and deep, then guided my head to a faster rhythm as he neared his release. Wanting to do even more for him, I swallowed him deeper and deeper, until he finally came with a tired groan, buried all the way in my throat.

Pulling my head back, he told me to lick him clean, and then gave me the order he had woken me up for.

"Go see about our luggage, Bethany," he ordered. "I want every item of clothing you packed last night to be taken out, laundered, dried, ironed, and re-packed before our flight."

I jerked in denial. *What?!* There was no reason--

Crack! His open hand whipped my head to the side with a resounding slap. Looking up at him respectfully, I was reminded that he didn't need a reason.

"Yes, sir," I answered. And then, finally remembering: "Thank you."

CHAPTER FOUR

O n the airplane, I wriggled uncomfortably in my seat. I had surrendered to full submission and had been obeying my husband without question ever since his 3:00 am reminder. But it didn't mean it was comfortable.

Richard had ordered me to wear a very short dress, with no panties or bra, and 4" heels. Sexy? Absolutely. But it was the middle of the morning and walking through the airport in these heels was ridiculous. Now that we were seated on the plane, I was freezing, my nipples pebbled tightly under the thin material and jutting forward to the delight of the man next to me, who kept sneaking glances at my tits.

Richard had seated me in the middle of a row of three, and the rough material of the seat abraded my sore, bruised bottom. The short, tight dress offered no protection, as it rode up to the crease of my thighs when I sat in the cramped quarters. I had to keep my legs firmly pressed together to avoid flashing anyone who cared to look with my shaved pussy.

I wanted so badly to complain, but realized of course that this was exactly why I needed training.

Richard had the window seat, and as soon as we took off he wrapped a proprietary hand around my upper thigh, forcing his fingers between my closed thighs.

"Spread your legs, Bethany," he ordered without bothering to lower his voice.

I was mortified. I could feel my face flaming as I furtively glanced at the man seated on the other side of me. He looked too young to be wearing the expensive suit he had on, and had lowered his tray table and pulled out a laptop as soon as he sat down.

Although with me seated next to him, he hadn't even glanced at the screen. He'd been unable to take his eyes off my quite obviously unbound tits and obscenely short skirt. At my husband's words, the man groaned quietly and shot a furtive glance at Richard.

Richard smiled at him as he dug his fingers painfully into my inner thigh. It was a quick reminder of our training, and reluctantly I did as I was told.

"Yes, sir," I remembered to say quietly.

My husband's hand on my thigh let me know that my efforts at modesty were going to be completely ignored. With a firm touch, he guided me to spread my legs as wide as I could. He wasn't satisfied until I had one knee pressed against each man's thigh.

The position forced my tight skirt all the way up over my hips, making it look like I was wearing nothing more than a tight, long shirt and heels. My face flamed with embarrassment as my smooth mound was put on full display.

"You don't mind, do you?" he asked the man in the suit.

"Um--"

His laptop bounced on the tray table, and I looked down to see his pants suddenly tented with a massive erection.

"My wife is in training," Richard went. He kept his eyes on the other man and spoke in a pleasant, conversational voice. He also started stroking my slit.

At his first touch, I was wet. I had conceded all ability to deny him. Obeying him without question was a kind of freedom I'd never known before, and because he was in charge, I could sit next to a total stranger getting blatantly fingered in public by my husband. And liking it.

I panted softly. Having the young businessman watch me was ratcheting up my arousal. He couldn't look away as Richard played with my clit and pushed a finger inside me. I lay my head back and panted softly, deliberately pressing my leg harder against the stranger as I tried to open my thighs even further.

"Wh-what kind of training?" he finally asked Richard, still mesmerized by my cunt.

"Bethany is learning to submit completely to my authority. She is practicing obeying me without question."

"Your wife... she'll do anything you tell her to?" his eyes darted briefly to mine and I smiled, subtly rubbing my knee against his thigh. Of course Richard noticed.

"Bethany," he admonished. "Stop teasing the young man. Or I'll make him part of your training."

My pussy clenched around the two fingers he now had inside me, and I know he felt the surge of slick excitement that his words caused.

"Yes, sir," I replied breathlessly.

"I see that you have work to do during the flight," Richard nodded toward the other man's laptop.

"N-no, nope. I'm totally available," the stranger said as he snapped the cover closed. "I would, uh, be happy to help with any training." He licked his lips and I could see his cock twitching under the tray table.

"Thank you," Richard said with a small smile. "Her training during the flight has to do with ownership. I own this sweet pussy. I will tell Bethany what to do with it, and when, and with whom. If you would be so kind--"

My husband pulled an 8" vibrating dildo from his briefcase and handed it to the man next to me. It looked exactly like a penis, but hot pink.

"Please fuck my wife with the dildo."

The man turned it on, and tentatively touched the tip to my wet cunt. It felt incredible. I pushed myself against it, angling my hips down to press my clit into the vibrating head.

I moaned, and couldn't stop myself from grabbing his wrist and trying to urge him closer. I wanted more.

"Bethany!" Richard said sharply. With a hard pinch to my nipple, my husband pulled my hand away. "You will not move unless I allow it."

"Yes, sir," I panted.

Bolder now, the stranger pushed the dildo inside me slowly. I tensed my sheath to magnify the sensation. Stifling a moan, I tried not to draw attention from the other passengers.

He pulled it out, and drove it in again. My slick juices were coating his hand as it bumped against me with his thrusts. Excited, he started pumping it in and out, faster and faster. Heat was coiling in my sex, and I could feel a massive orgasm coming like a tidal wave. Panting openly, I threw my head back against the seat and then--

"Stop."

Richard pulled the stranger's hand away. I had to bite my lip and fight not to thrust my own hands between my legs. Frustration slammed through me and my hips involuntarily arched off the seat, looking for more.

"Bethany, you will not come unless I give you permission."

"Yes, sir," I managed to say. "Please…"

Richard turned to our seat mate. The man was still staring at my sopping cunt, holding the pink dildo as if he had forgotten about it. Sweat beaded his brow and his hands were clenched tightly.

"That will be all we need from you," my husband said to him as he plucked the sex toy out of his hand and wrapped it in a small towel. "If you'd like to wait in the onboard restroom, I will send Bethany to you so that she can thank you for your training."

My pussy clenched in excitement.

Richard's hand held me firmly in place as the stranger scrambled out of his seat and headed to the back of the plane.

"Bethany," he smiled at me softly. "Go to him and take care of his needs in whatever way he requires. But you are my wife, and there will be punishment later for having another man touch you. Please keep that in mind."

I sucked in a sharp breath. But of course. I exhaled. What better way to train me that I was under his complete control, then to order me to do something for which I would be punished later?

"Yes, sir," I answered dutifully. "Do I have permission for an orgasm, sir?"

When I squeezed into the tiny bathroom with the man who had masturbated me, there was barely room for us to both stand. His straining cock stabbed into my lower back as I turned to close and lock the folding door. Immediately, his hands were on my firm breasts, squeezing them tightly and pinching my nipples in a way that made me almost come just standing there. Thank God Richard had said yes.

"Are-are you really okay with this?" he asked hesitantly while he ground his erection into me from behind.

Turning to face him, I rubbed myself against him in the cramped space and smiled up at him. His cock was now pressed into my belly, and I wanted it inside me so badly I thought I would scream.

"I have no choice," I answered as I unzipped him. "Now, would you like to fuck me?"

He lifted me onto the tiny sink and drove his thick shaft into me as soon as I freed it. Wrapping my legs around his hips, I ground myself against him and came, hard, with his first thrust.

"You. Are. So. Fucking. Hot," he ground out as my pussy clamped down around him with my orgasm. "I'm going to make you come again, you little slut."

He slipped his hands under my ass as he pounded into me, and I knew I had to do as he said. His cock was hitting me just right and another orgasm started to build as soon as the first one faded.

"Fuck!" he shouted. "I'm going to come! You're going to come, too. Now!" he shoved a finger deep into my ass as he filled me with hot spurts of cum, and I screamed as I exploded again. Obeying his command.

CHAPTER FIVE

A s soon as we landed, my husband led me into a "family restroom". Placing my hands on the sink, he bent me over and pushed my dress up to my waist. The stranger's sticky cum was smeared on my thighs, and Richard spread my legs apart for a better look.

"Did you like it when he fucked you, Bethany?"

"Yes, sir," I watched in the mirror as he pulled a wooden paddle out of his briefcase.

Crack!

He brought it down hard on the crease at the top of my legs. Crack! The next one hit my left cheek.

And another. And another. I didn't bother counting, just watched myself in the little mirror as my face reddened and tears poured down my cheeks.

"Thank you, sir," I repeated after each strike. When he finally finished, I washed my face and my pussy, then sighed in contentment as he pulled me into his arms.

Kissing me softly, he whispered how proud he was of my total submission. I had never been as in love with him as I was at that moment. Giving in completely was a heady feeling, and I was humbled by how far he was willing to go in order to train me properly.

I dropped to my knees and thanked him properly. As I swallowed his sweet cum I few minutes later, I smiled in anticipation. I wondered what he had planned for the rest of my training...

BETHANY'S SUBMISSION - PART 2

A DOMESTIC DISCIPLINE SPANKING ROMANCE

CHAPTER ONE

The second day of my submission training started earlier than I had expected. My husband Richard had set an alarm that went off on my phone at 4:00 a.m. He'd turned the volume down and left it on the hotel night table next to my pillow, so he slept right through it when it went off.

Strip, and wait for me in the bathroom. Place your hands on the counter and bend over in spanking position. Do not move until given permission. Richard had set up the alarm to display his message when it sounded.

Careful not to disturb him, I rolled out of bed and removed my nightgown and panties. The bathroom was dark. I kept the light off so it didn't disturb his sleep and followed his instructions.

I knew he was planning on getting up early to prepare for the day's board meeting, but that still meant I had at least an hour to stand naked and bent over in front of the darkened bathroom mirror.

I stifled a tired sigh. I had agreed to submit to his authority in every way, and I reminded myself that this meant even within my own head. So instead of focusing on how tired I was, I turned my thoughts to the day before. My first day of training.

During our flight, Richard had treated me like a sex toy. Despite my embarrassment, the freedom of having no choice and allowing him to use me as he saw fit had been both erotic and freeing.

He had enlisted the help of a stranger to teach me utter submission, allowing the man seated with us to use me however he needed. The memory of getting fucked at my husband's command in the airplane bathroom had my pussy tingling within moments. I pressed my thighs together, wishing I could touch myself.

Richard and I had been practicing a Domestic Discipline lifestyle for several years. It had vastly improved our marriage, but until now, I had constantly struggled with my role as a submissive wife.

Before agreeing to learn submission through this Boot Camp style training, I had constantly forgotten my place, made silly mistakes, broken my husband's rules, and gotten soundly spanked and punished for it on a regular basis. I *wanted* to submit to his authority as Head of our Household, but somehow I could never quite let go and fully *do* it.

When Richard found a Domestic Discipline boot camp online, it sounded like the perfect answer. It was designed as submissiveness training for wives new to the lifestyle... but unfortunately it started this week, the same week that my husband had to fly out of town for a board meeting.

Since we couldn't make the Boot Camp, he decided to bring me along on his business trip. And he designed a training program of his own.

I have found that *anything* can be mastered with training, practice, and repetition. It's how I became a professional ballerina years ago, how I learned French in my 20's, and now - I hoped - how I would finally learn to be the truly submissive wife that my husband deserved.

With my whole hearted consent, I agreed that he would own me, completely, during this trip. He didn't need or want me to be a slave forever, but hopefully by the time my training ended I would have learned to submit to his authority as naturally as breathing. It would definitely make our marriage run more smoothly.

Being able to sit without wincing would also be a perk. Before training, he used to have to spank me a *lot*.

Actually, he was still spanking me a lot. But that was part of the training. My maintenance spankings every morning and every night helped me remember that he was in charge of me.

I was also required to give him a formal "thank you" after every punishment, which meant I was sucking his cock several times a day. And of course, I had to obey him completely.

It wasn't up to me to wonder why he had me to do the things he commanded. My job was simply to submit, without question or hesitation, to *anything* he ordered me to do. And to endure it, if necessary. Occasionally enjoying it was just a perk.

I shivered again as I remembered the pleasure that obeying him had given me the day before.

"Good morning, Bee," Richard said sleepily behind me.

I had been so lost in my thoughts that I hadn't even heard his alarm go off. He had flipped on the bathroom light before I realized he was there, and I met his eyes in the mirror as he smiled. He let his eyes rove up and down my naked body as I patiently held the submissive position he had instructed me to assume.

Tenderly stroking his hands over the welts from last night's spanking, he spread my legs wider and reached between them to finger my cunt. He smiled even wider when he felt how wet I was. And of course I wasn't going to tell him that it was the memory of yesterday's mile high initiation that had done it.

Pulling his thickening cock out of his boxers, he slid it between my thighs and stroked himself against my damp slit until he got fully hard. Then he held me firmly by the hips and pushed himself in, long and slow.

I watched in the mirror. The sight of him pumping into me from behind was almost as good as the feel.

He was only half awake, and the whole time I watched he kept his eyes pointed down at the action.

He seemed mesmerized by the sight of his cock sliding in and out of my wet hole. Moving his hands from my hips to my ass, he spread me wider and started stroking up and down my crack. Every time his fingers passed over my little back hole, I shivered.

The stranger who had fucked me yesterday had pushed his finger deep into my anus the second time he'd made me come, and it had taken my orgasm to heights I had never experienced before. For all the attention that Richard usually gave my ass, he had never done anything like that. I was an anal virgin. Well, except for that guy's delicious finger.

Now that I'd had a taste, I wanted more.

My husband's fingers playing *right there* as he fucked me made me moan with need. I pushed back against him, hoping he would slip one inside me. Instead, he reached around me and pinched my nipples, sending a jolt straight down to my cunt.

Just as I felt my body tightening, Richard straightened up suddenly and stared hard into my eyes in the mirror.

"You are not. Allowed. To come, Bethany," he ground out between his thrusts. "If you come. Without my.

Permission. Your morning. Spanking. Will be. With the cane. Instead. Of. The. Paddle."

I scraped my nails against the hard counter top in frustration as I watched him let go. His fingers dug into my hips as he came, and he held my stare the whole time as if daring me to disobey. My cunt was screaming for release, but with panting breaths I struggled to do as I was told.

"Don't move. Don't come," he ordered as he pulled out and stepped into the shower behind me.

My whole body was throbbing with sexual frustration as I continued to lean over the counter, holding position until he told me otherwise. I craved my morning spanking. Hopefully the wooden paddle he favored would help release some of my tension.

Once he was dressed, he came back to take care of me.

Crack!

The first blow drove me forward, and I bit my lip to stop from crying out. Spankings were usually something I anticipated with eyes tightly closed. I had never had to watch as he swung that horrible slab of wood through the air. I'd never had to see my flesh trembling as it slammed into my ass.

My interrupted orgasm was forgotten.

My whole body got hot, and I knew my bottom was as red as I could see my face getting. By the tenth strike against my bruised and tender flesh, I was crying.

I had consented to his utter authority, and as I watched myself get spanked I realized that I wasn't trying to get away. True, I couldn't help flinching and sobbing as my body reacted to the fiery pain. But he chose to do it, and that by itself made it right. *This must be what submission feels like.*

I was his. Utterly.

CHAPTER TWO

I was wearing a short wrap around dress that closed only by tying around my waist. Richard had chosen it for me, and just as he had the day before, he instructed me not to wear a bra or panties.

"I own your body, Bethany," he reminded me. "Today you will come to the board meeting with me, and you will give me access to any part of you that I request, at any time. This dress will make that easy."

Before we had left the hotel room, he'd had me practice opening the dress with one pull of the tie, and holding the front open for him so that he could see and touch my body. I quickly learned to open it easily and quickly, and to retie it just as fast.

In the cab ride over, he'd ordered me to pull my breasts out of the low top so that he could enjoy them. He'd idly fondled them as the cab driver stole glances in the rearview mirror. I don't know whether I was more turned on by his touch, or by knowing the cabby was watching.

Despite not being allowed to come, I was enjoying my training more than I would have believed possible. The freedom of having to do whatever he told me quelled all my inhibitions, and I reveled in the exhibitionism.

When we arrived at the Cummington Group headquarters, we checked in at the lobby, then got in the elevator for the ride to the 30th floor. Just as the doors were closing, a tall man who looked vaguely familiar caught them and joined us.

"Richard, good to see you," he said as he pumped my husband's hands. "And-- is this Barbara?"

"Bethany, my wife," Richard corrected with a smile. "How have you been, Declan?"

"Not bad," the other man said. "Especially since my divorce finally went through!"

"I'm sorry to hear that," my husband responded.

Declan was shaking his head with a smile before Richard finished talking. He didn't look at all sorry, and put a hand up to stop any more words of sympathy.

"Really, it's for the best. My ex was... difficult," he sighed. "Life is truly much better without having to bear *that*. No offense, Barbara."

Richard looked at him, assessing him for a moment, then smiled.

"*Bethany*," he emphasized my name slightly. "Please turn around and lift your dress."

Without hesitating, I did as I was told. Pulling the short skirt up to my waist, I spread my legs and arched my back so that my tight, round bottom was thrust toward the two men.

The sight of my naked ask made Declan suck in a sharp breath. My curvy skin was blotched with fading bruises and healing welts, and still had a pleasant pinkness to it from my morning spanking.

"This is why I don't have those kind of problems," Richard said.

I felt a hand stroke my ass, and idly wondered which man had touched me.

"When my wife gets out of line, she gets punished. And when she does as she's told, she still has a couple of daily spankings so that she doesn't forget who is in charge."

"Is she always this... compliant?" Declan asked.

Richard laughed. I wondered if he was remembering what he had ordered me to do yesterday on the plane. And then I wondered if he would order me to do something like that again. My pussy was suddenly wet, reminding me vividly of the fact that I hadn't been allowed to come this morning.

"She will do absolutely anything I tell her to do," he said confidently. I glowed with his praise.

"Show me," Declan said after a long pause. I pictured my husband's smile.

"Bethany, until I say otherwise, you will obey Declan as you would obey me. Is that understood?"

"Yes, sir," I replied promptly.

"Try it out," I could hear the smile in my husband's voice as he offered me to the other man. My heart started racing with excitement, wondering what Declan would do with me.

"Um, what-- what should I ask her to do?" he asked hesitantly.

"What do you *want* her to do?" My husband promptly responded. And then I felt a lurch and realized that he'd stopped the elevator, giving the three of us time for whatever Declan decided. Richard chuckled and added: "Anything goes, Declan."

"Um, okay. Bar-Bethany, please turn around," he finally said.

When I turned and faced him I immediately noticed the bulge in his pants. Smiling, I made sure that he saw me looking.

"Lift your dress again," he ordered with a gulp.

"Yes, sir," I said softly as I complied.

His dick twitched hard under his tented pants as he looked at my shaved cunt. When he didn't tell me to do anything else, I spread my legs a bit and pushed my pelvis toward him.

"Do you want to touch her, Declan?" Richard finally asked.

Without answering, Declan lurched toward me and used one finger to trace the slick slit that parted my mound. Pulling his finger back, he rubbed the moist digit with his thumb. When neither Richard nor I protested, he got bolder.

Declan stepped closer to me. He reached down and palmed my pussy with his right hand, driving his middle finger up into my wet hole. He grabbed my ass with the other hand and squeezed the sore flesh tightly, causing me to gasp.

"Do you like that?" he whispered.

"Yes, sir," I answered with a smile. I tightened the walls of my pussy around his thick finger. "Very much."

Declan groaned, and pushed all four fingers into me without warning. I ground against his hand, all the tension of my husband's morning fuck flooding back down to my cunt in an instant.

"Bethany!" Richard said sharply. "Remember that you have not been given permission to come."

At the sound of my husband's voice, Declan jumped back, looking guilty. Richard quickly reassured him.

"Please, feel free to continue, Declan."

"Can I-- can I get her to suck my cock?" Declan asked tentatively.

I was already dropping to my knees as my husband nodded. Declan's hands fumbled at his belt, and he finally pulled his erection out and clumsily pushed it toward my face.

Wrapping my lips around him eagerly, I heard him groan as his hands came to rest softly on my shoulders. His penis was thick, but shorter than my husbands. I had no trouble taking all of him, and sucked him greedily as Richard watched.

Declan was clearly not the take charge type, and after a moment Richard stepped up behind me and held my head firmly.

"Faster, Bethany," he ordered. And then to Declan, "Sorry to jump in, but the board meeting starts in ten minutes."

Submitting to his hands just as I would to any order, I let Richard pump my head on the other man's cock. I braced myself with one hand on Declan's hip and the other holding the base of his shaft.

"Oh fuck!" Declan hissed as Richard forced me to suck him hard and fast. "Fuuuuccccckkkkkkk!"

Declan slammed his hands against the elevator walls to steady himself as his hips jerked toward me. Hot cum shot down my throat and I sucked him like a straw until he was empty.

"Lick him clean," Richard reminded me.

As soon as Declan had himself tucked in, Richard restarted the elevator.

"Um, thank you?" Declan looked uncertainly between Richard and me. Now that I'd gotten him off, he seemed awkward and eager to get away from us. He bolted out of the elevator doors as soon as they opened, and Richard and I turned to each other and burst out laughing.

"I do love you, Bee," he pulled me to him for a quick kiss, but then thought better of it. He swatted my ass instead and then gave me a little push.

"Go find some mouthwash, and clean yourself up. We should have a break sometime in the next couple of hours. During the break, I'm going to watch you masturbate until you come, as reward for your perfect submission today."

Excited, I reached up to kiss him and then remembered that I couldn't. Laughing, I apologized.

"Thank you, sir," I smiled appreciatively. "You are so good to me."

"And don't think I haven't noticed how much you enjoy being watched, and used by other men," he whispered to me as a couple of executives walked past us into the boardroom.

"Yes, sir," I admitted. I knew this meant he would punish me later. And I smiled wider as I realized that it didn't matter. I would do what he ordered, no matter what. And when he punished me for doing as I was told, I would thank him for it.

Shivering in wicked delight, I watched my husband walk away and started counting down the minutes until he returned to continue my training.

BETHANY'S SUBMISSION - PART 3

A DOMESTIC DISCIPLINE SPANKING ROMANCE

CHAPTER ONE

I was laying on my back with my knees bent, fingering myself with one hand while I frantically rubbed my clit with the other.

"Spread your legs wider, Bethany," my husband, Richard, ordered.

"Yes, sir."

Doing as I was told had finally become second nature. After struggling with my role as the submissive wife for the past few years of our Domestic Discipline marriage, Richard had brought me on a business trip with him and designed a Boot Camp style submissiveness training program for me. And it was working.

It was the middle of the morning, and he was finally rewarding me for my perfect obedience by letting me come. He'd already punished me, fucked me, and let another man use me today, but I had been under strict orders... Do. Not. Come.

My pussy spasmed around my wet fingers as my orgasm finally ripped through me. I screamed as my hips jerked up off the smooth top of the executive desk he'd ordered me to lie back on. I was so caught up in the delicious feeling coursing through me that I didn't even hear the office door open.

"What the hell?!"

I didn't bother to move. The best thing about submission was that I *had* to do as I was told. I felt no shame as I lay on a stranger's desk with my wet cunt on display. My husband had ordered it, and that trumped all other considerations.

"Richard, what-- what's going on here?"

"Arnie, good morning," he said pleasantly. And then to me: "Bethany, go clean yourself up and then come back in here."

Sliding off the desk, I saw a distinguished, silver haired man in a very expensive suit staring at me in shock. And not just shock. I dropped my eyes to his package as I brushed past him, and tried to hide a small smile when I saw a telltale bulge.

He looked familiar. As I washed my hands and wiped the slippery evidence of my excitement off my thighs in the restroom, it finally came to me. He was Arnold Davis, President and CEO of Cummington Group.

Mr. Davis was staring out his wall to wall windows when I returned to his spacious corner office, and I took a moment to admire the fit, older man from the rear. I idly wondered what my husband had told him about my erotic display.

"Bethany, lock the door," Richard ordered me as I came in. "Mr. Davis has agreed to let us continue to use his office. In exchange for which he would like to participate in your punishment."

I shivered. I had given my husband absolute authority over me. It wasn't my place to question what he chose to do with me. Or who he chose to have do it. It was simply my place to obey.

"Take your dress off, Bethany, then bend over and hold your ankles."

"Yes, sir."

Richard had chosen a short, wrap around dress for me today that gave easy access to my body. The top was cut low and he didn't allow me to wear any bra or panties. It could also be opened and closed with just one tug on the tie that wrapped around my slim waist.

Mr. Davis had turned to watch. I liked being watched.

Turning toward him, I slowly pulled the tie open and let the dress spread apart. I had been a professional ballerina in my late teens and twenties, and my body still had the long lines and firm muscle tone from my early career. When I stopped dancing, I was finally able to add a womanly curviness that men couldn't seem to resist.

My tits were still a high and firm C cup, and at the moment sported very tight, pebbled nipples. I saw the older man glance at them, but then his eyes dropped to my shaved mound. It was still pink and swollen from masturbating on his desk.

Letting my dress fall to the floor, I turned around so that he had a good view of my backside, then bent over to grab my ankles as my husband had ordered. I wondered if he liked what he saw.

I had my legs spread just enough to give him a good view of my moist slit. It was framed by my tight ass, still blotched with fading bruises and healing welts from the spankings my husband had given me over the last few days.

"Bethany gave oral sex to another man this morning. She's earned a spanking," my husband old the other man.

Richard walked up behind me and stroked my ass gently. He let his fingers trail down to my pussy and slipped one inside absentmindedly.

"You're welcome to use your bare hand, Arnie, or I've brought a paddle."

Mr. Davis walked over to stand next to my husband. I felt his sweaty hand stroke my flank, and the feel of both men touching me at once excited me. Richard continued to finger me while the CEO rubbed one hand up and down my ass. He wedged his thumb into my crack so that it pressed on my tight little star with every stroke.

I knew I wasn't supposed to move without asking, but I couldn't help pushing myself against their fingers. I wanted more. Mr. Davis laughed.

"She's a hot one, isn't she, Richard?"

"Hot, and willing. She's in training right now, and obeys me without question."

Bent over as I was, all I could see of the two men were there legs. And their cocks. Both had obvious bulges, and I saw Mr. Davis' jerk under his suit pants at my husband's words.

"I'll pass on the paddle. I want to start with my bare hand," he said as he squeezed my firm cheek.

Richard stepped out of the way, and Mr. Davis smacked his hand down on my ass. With nothing to support me, the blow rocked me forward.

"I've got you, Sweetheart," he said in a low, excited voice.

He slid one hand under my stomach and slipped it down my body until he was palming my mound. Holding me steady with that hand as he blatantly fingered my slit, he spanked me hard with the other.

Despite lots of stimulation over the course of the morning, Richard had forbidden me to come until the moment he ordered me to masturbate for him on the CEO's desk. I had needed it, but it still hadn't been able to fully satisfy me after so long in a state of intense arousal.

Now, the combination of pleasure/pain that Mr. Davis was giving me was going to give me a second orgasm if I didn't watch out. Just because my husband had allowed me to come once, I knew that didn't mean I could do it again without his permission. But oooooooh. I wanted to.

I squeezed my pussy tight around Mr. Davis' fingers, enjoying the erotic surge that pulsed through me every time his other hand landed on my ass with an echoing slap.

From the throbbing heat in my ass, I knew it had to be bright red, but Mr. Davis showed no signs of stopping. His hard cock was pressed into my thigh, and I subtly shifted my weight to rub against it. Of course Richard saw.

"Hold up, Arnie," my husband commanded.

Reluctantly pulling his fingers out of my cunt, Mr. Davis stepped back.

"She's enjoying that a little too much," Richard chuckled. "This is supposed to be punishment. Would you mind continuing with your belt?"

I recognized the soft hiss of a leather belt being pulled out of its belt loops. No matter how horny I was, I knew better than to think this part would be fun.

His belt slapped into my ass with a streak of fiery pain. There was no more "holding me up", so I had to tense my muscles to take it without falling forward. Mr. Davis was really getting into it, and the belt lit into me over and over, until tears were streaming down my face.

His aim left something to be desired, and the strikes were all over the place. The ones that licked across my pussy made me flinch and cry out, but I trusted that Richard knew that was involuntary. Despite the pain, I was happy to take it. Because my husband had ordered it.

When Mr. Davis finally stopped, my lower body ached with a burning, fiery pain. I knew my face had to be red as well, and probably blotchy with tears. I could hear the CEO breathing hard behind me. Richard hadn't said a word while he whipped me with his belt, and I wondered why he'd stopped.

"Holy shit, Richard," he finally panted. "That's almost better than sex. She just took whatever I gave her."

I imagined my husband nodding, and smiling with pride. I loved being able to demonstrate his mastery over me to others.

"Bethany, your punishment is complete. Please thank Mr. Davis for the discipline."

Standing up stiffly, I turned to face the two men. The CEO was flushed, and looked slightly disheveled from the effort he'd made to correct me. I knew that sucking his cock as a formal thank you would help settle him down, and I was eager to do it.

Before I could approach him, he glanced down at his watch and frowned.

"I lost track of time, Richard," he said. "The board meeting resumes in a couple of minutes."

"She can be a bit distracting," my husband replied with a chuckle. "Arnie, do you mind if I leave her in your office until we break for lunch? Since we don't have time for her to thank you properly, I want to make sure you have access to her later in the day."

Mr. Davis looked me up and down with a hot smile. I could tell he didn't know what my husband meant about "thanking him properly", but he obviously liked the idea of having access to me.

"Of course," he said easily. "So as long as you don't mind leaving her locked in... I wouldn't want anyone to accidentally walk in on her like this. My secretary has the only other key."

The two men agreed, and Mr. Davis handed Richard his key. The CEO left to freshen himself up before the meeting and my husband came to me and kissed me tenderly.

"I'm so proud of you, Bee," he told me lovingly. His approval wrapped around me like a warm blanket.

He led me over to the corner, and pulled a bag of white rice out of his briefcase. He laid the large, flat desk blotter from the CEO's desk down on the carpet, and liberally sprinkled the rice over it.

"Bethany, you will kneel on the rice with your fingers laced on top of your head until I return. You will not dress, or lower your hands, or move from this spot without my permission. Is that clear?"

"Yes, sir," I answered as I assumed the position.

His footsteps were muffled by the carpet, but I heard the click of the lock turning as he closed the door and left. The corner he had left me in was completely unadorned, and I tried to think of something pleasant while I waited.

My ass was still burning with a stinging, buzzing ache from the belt, and the tiny uncooked grains of rice bit into my knees like angry spiders. I sighed contentedly. Every little stab of pain brought me happiness.

I'm no glutton for punishment, but I loved submitting to my husband's will. He owned me, and obeying him without question had taught me a deep contentment I'd never felt before.

I heard the lock click behind me, and started in surprise. I assumed Richard would be gone for at least a couple of hours, and it didn't seem possible that that much time had passed.

"Oh my *God!*"

I didn't even flinch. The feminine voice behind me didn't belong to my husband, therefore I didn't need to react to it.

She rushed over to me, and I felt the softness of her hand on my shoulder.

"Who-- What-- What's going on?"

I turned my head slightly, hoping that didn't violate my husband's not moving rule. I saw an attractive woman of about 40, dressed in a conservative business suit and low heels.

"Get up! You can't be-be *naked*. This is Mr. Davis' office! The CEO! What are you doing here?"

She pulled on my shoulder as the words tumbled out of her mouth, and I had to use all my years of strength training to hold my position against her frantically tugging hands.

"Mr. Davis is aware I'm here," I told her calmly. "I'm not allowed to move until my husband returns, so please-- would you take your hands off me? You're going to make me lose my balance."

Shocked into immobility, she stared at me for a moment before rushing back to close and lock the door. She took a moment to compose herself, and then came back over to the corner. Managing to work her way between me and the wall, she crouched down to look me in the eye.

"Okay. I've guaranteed some privacy. I am Mr. Davis' executive secretary, and I have trouble believing that he-- condones this... totally inappropriate display. Please explain to me what's going on." She pursed her lips disapprovingly and let her eyes drift down over my exposed body.

"My husband is attending the board meeting," I explained. "He has ordered me to stay here until he and Mr. Davis return."

"*Ordered* you?" she asked skeptically. "Are you some kind of sex slave?"

I wasn't, technically. I was simply a submissive wife. But I can't deny that I enjoyed my husband using me

- and letting others use me - during my training. The thought aroused me as it always did, and I watched as the woman's eyes moved down to my breasts. The nipples had hardened at the words "sex slave".

I smiled at her without answering.

"The men won't be out of the meeting for another two hours," she said thoughtfully. "You're really going to kneel here, naked, for that entire time?"

"Yes, ma'am," I answered dutifully.

She reached out and put a hand on my shoulder. Her touch made my breath quicken, and I realized I had become a slut for the touch of strangers.

"What, exactly, are you required to do?"

"At the moment, I just have to stay here. I'm not allowed to move from this position, or to move my hands, or to dress, until my husband returns."

Keeping her eyes on me, she ran her hand down over my chest and cupped one of my breasts. Kneading the firm mound gently in her hand, she took the nipple between her fingers and rolled it.

Instantly, I was turned on. My back arched as I pressed into her touch.

"You liked that."

It wasn't a question, but I answered anyway, hoping she would do more.

"Yes, ma'am."

"So... you are so obedient, that you won't move, no matter what I do to you?"

"Yes, ma'am."

She suddenly pinched my nipple and gave it a painful twist. Tears sprung to my eyes, but I didn't pull away.

"Oh my," she said thoughtfully.

She slid a hand down my taut stomach and ran her finger through my wet slit. She smiled devilishly when she felt the evidence of my excitement, and pushed a finger up inside me.

"You really are a sex slave," she said in wonder.

"Yes, ma'am," I replied happily as she fingered me. My husband had not given me permission to come. But he also hadn't forbidden it. I ground my mound against her hand and she started to finger fuck me harder.

"You little slut," she laughed. "You want me to make you come, don't you?"

"Yes, ma'am. Please," I begged as her finger hit my g-spot. I moaned in pleasure.

"No," she said evilly as she pulled her hand away. "If you're willing to subjugate yourself like this, I don't know that you deserve it. But that doesn't mean I won't put you to work."

She stood up and unzipped her skirt. Letting it fall to the floor, she stepped out of it and pulled her lace panties off. The sheer, thigh high stockings she wore surprised me. I had never been attracted to a woman before, but the way they framed her pale, shaved muff was incredibly sexy.

Or maybe I just thought so because she'd had her fingers buried in my cunt.

"I can't move my hands, ma'am," I told her breathlessly.

"That's ok," she replied. "I only need your tongue."

She stepped up to me and pushed my face against her pussy. I'd tasted my own juice on my husband's cock, but her flavor was different. Muskier. I stretched my tongue out and slid it up her slit.

"That's right," she sighed huskily. "Now suck my clit."

I found her swollen nub and sucked it into my mouth. It was tiny compared to a man's penis, but the same principles applied. I circled it with my tongue and sucked it gently. But she didn't want gentle.

Her hands were on the back of my head and she ground against me, rubbing herself up and down on my busy tongue. I wished I had permission to move my hands so that I could part her folds and lick her deeper, but I didn't dare disobey the direct order I'd been given.

"Oh fuck," she sighed when I returned to sucking her clit. "That's right, slut. Faster!"

I obeyed. She was riding my face with abandon, and her little cries of pleasure were making my own pussy ache to be fucked.

"Oh my God! Suck *harder*, slut, *faster*!" she screamed at me.

I sucked her like a kid desperate to get to the center of a lollipop, using my chin to rub against her cunt as I worked hard on her clit.

Finally, with a high pitched squeal, she pulled my hair and came all over my face.

After she'd caught her breath, the satisfied woman got dressed silently. She gave my nipple another hard pinch once she'd put herself back together, then reached down to brush a light kiss across my lips. Her musky juice was drying on my face, and I could smell her with every breath I took.

"That was a nice mid-morning treat," she praised me with a smile. "Be sure you treat my boss just as well."

I heard the soft click of the door and the lock turning behind me as she left. I was so horny it almost hurt. Thank God I had the pain from the rice and the belt to take my attention off of my needy pussy.

I waited patiently, breathing in the scent of the other woman's orgasm and silently praying for my husband's return. I didn't care if he made me stay down on this rice all day. I only hoped he'd bend me over and fuck me, hard and fast, when he got back.

I really, really, really wanted to come.

BETHANY'S SUBMISSION - PART 4

A DOMESTIC DISCIPLINE SPANKING ROMANCE

CHAPTER ONE

My husband, Richard, was taking me to lunch at an upscale restaurant near the headquarters of the Cummington Group. He hadn't yet let me know whether I would be allowed to eat, but honestly, that was less important to me at the moment than when I would get my next orgasm.

It was my second day of submissiveness training, and after providing oral service to both the CEO after the morning board meeting session and his executive secretary earlier in the morning, I was restless and sexually frustrated as we walked into the restaurant.

Richard and I had been living a Domestic Discipline lifestyle for several years, but it wasn't until he brought me on this business trip with him that I was finally able to fully submit to his authority.

I had always *wanted* to, but something inside me had struggled with submission from the beginning. I had wholeheartedly agreed that Richard should wear the pants in the family from the moment I'd said "I do", but despite that I had constantly forgotten my place, made silly mistakes, broken Richard's rules, and seemed to walk around with a bruised, aching bottom from well deserved spankings every day of the week.

Before we flew out here, my husband had designed a Boot Camp style submissiveness training program for me that required me to obey him absolutely, without question or hesitation, during this trip. Apparently, that's exactly what I had needed.

When I finally surrendered to the fact that his will trumped mine, unconditionally, my life became easy. There was a freedom that came with having no choice in the matter. When Richard ordered me to do something, I simply did it. His will was my gravity. Inescapable.

Arnold Davis, the President and CEO of Cummington Group and the man whose cock I had

had in my mouth a short time ago, was coming to lunch with us. My husband had told Mr. Davis about my training, and even allowed the CEO to help administer my punishment after the other man had walked in on me masturbating -- upon my husband's orders -- in his office.

I think Mr. Davis had enjoyed spanking me with his leather belt even more than my formal thank you afterward.

Mr. Davis kept stealing glances at me as we got out of the cab and entered the restaurant. I was wearing a short, wrap around dress that my husband had chosen for me because it gave him easy access to my body. It had a loose skirt, a low cut top, and just one tie around that waist to hold it closed. Richard hadn't allowed me to wear any bra or panties, and both he and Mr. Davis had taken turns fingering me during the cab ride over.

"Are you planning on continuing with your wife's training during lunch, Richard?" the CEO asked my husband excitedly as we walked in.

"Of course," Richard replied with a small smile. A little shiver ran through me.

While the hostess led Mr. Davis and I to a table, my husband stayed back to have a quiet conversation with the maitre d'. When he finally joined us at the table he handed me a small, wrapped gift box.

"Open it, sweetheart," he ordered. "I had Mr. Davis' secretary pick it up for you this morning.

I blushed. I hadn't told Richard that the other woman had walked in on me naked and used me herself while the men were occupied with the board meeting. I wondered if she had said anything to him. And whether I might be punished for it later.

Pulling the thick satin ribbon off the little box, I pulled the top off to reveal-- I didn't know what it was. It was a bright, shiny silver object about 4" long. One end was a flat circular shape inset with a blue jewel. If I stood it on the flat jeweled end, it would almost look like a cartoon tree, with a short, skinny "trunk" and an oval, ridged top that flared out and then narrowed to a rounded point at the end.

I pulled it out and looked at it curiously, waiting for Richard to tell me what to do with it. I glanced up at the two men, and saw that Mr. Davis was flushed with excitement.

"Bethany, that is your anal plug. You will be wearing it for the rest of the day, to prepare your body to be used later tonight."

My pussy clenched tightly at his words. Anal sex! Richard had never seemed interested in it before, but I have to admit that the thought had crossed my mind more than once over the last few years. Every time my husband had me bare and bent over for a spanking, I knew that my pink, puckering hole was winking back at him. Inviting him in. I bit back a smile. I guess he was finally ready to accept the invitation.

"Should I go insert it now, sir?" I asked hopefully.

"No," he replied as he leaned back in his chair.

My husband gave me a calculating look, and then glanced around the restaurant. Since it was lunch time, almost every table was filled with high powered executives and the clients they were wooing. The tables were spread far enough apart that each group was able to have a degree of privacy to conduct their business, and Richard kept his voice low as he gave me my instructions.

"Bethany, you've done very well at obeying me on this trip, and I no longer have any doubt that you are able to submit completely to my authority." I preened a bit under his praise. "But there will be times when you will have to think for yourself. Sometimes, I will need you to follow the intent of my orders without me giving you step by step instructions."

"Yes, sir."

"I need to know that I can trust you to follow an order, whether or not I'm there to tell you how to go about doing it," he continued. "While Arnie and I enjoy lunch, I'm going to give you specific instructions on *what* I want you to do, and then leave it up to you to figure out how to get it done. Is that clear?"

"Yes, sir," I responded eagerly. "What is it you want me to do?"

"We have an hour before we have to head back to the office. During that time, you will get one of the other diners to insert that plug for you. Do whatever it takes to get it done, or there will be severe consequences. My only guidelines are that you aren't to make a scene, and that I will need to verify it's inserted once you're done it."

My heart started to race as I looked around the room at the other men and women eating. I had no idea how I would approach a total stranger with such a bizarre request, but I knew that I had to do it on my husband's orders.

"I'll order for you and have a salad waiting. If you're able to get it done quickly, you'll be allowed to eat before we leave, but don't return to this table until it's done," he told me sternly.

"Yes, sir," I replied as I picked up the silver plug and pushed back my chair.

"One more thing, Bee," he said softly. "I trust you, but just to be sure, I've asked the maitre d' to provide a busboy to shadow you and report back to me."

Richard glanced over my shoulder and I turned. A young man in the white pants and jacket worn by the staff was standing directly behind me. He was probably about 20 years old, and looked nervous and excited. I noticed a bulge in his pants, and wondered what exactly he'd been told.

"This is Josh. He will be able to confirm which of the other diners you enlist for help, and tell me the details about how you accomplish it. And he also knows that there will be a generous tip for his service and discretion."

"Rich-- Sir, just to make sure I understand, you're telling me that Josh is supposed to... watch?"

"That's right, Bethany," Richard answered while glancing at his watch. "And you have 50 minutes left to get this done, so I suggest you get started."

CHAPTER TWO

I'd left the table and walked slowly through the dining area to a private hallway with discreet restrooms at the back of the restaurant. Josh trailed behind me, and I casually checked out the other diners as I passed through. Once we were in the relative privacy of the hallway, I turned to Josh with a smile.

"Josh, can you please tell me the exact instructions you were given?"

He licked his lips and blushed, his eyes dropping to my tits for a second before returning to my face.

"Um, ma'am, Bernie-- that is, the maitre d', he told me that, uh, your husband..." he trailed off uncertainly. "Is this-- is this all a joke?"

I didn't have a lot of time, so instead of answering him with words I gave a little tug to the tie holding my dress closed. The silky material fell open silently, and I pulled it away from my body like a central park flasher.

"No joke, Josh," I answered as my nipples puckered in excitement. "My husband has given me an order, and I need to obey it."

He couldn't take his eyes off my body. I could see his fingers twitch at his sides, as if he wanted to grab the generous mounds of my full, firm breasts. His gaze was drawn down to my smooth, hairless cunt, and the bulge in his pants suddenly flared into a rock hard erection that tented the front of his uniform a respectable 6" out in front of his body.

"Bernie told me that I was to stick with you, and watch as you have another customer put-- put something in your butt," he told me in a rush. Dragging his eyes up to mine for a split second, he asked eagerly, "Can I be the one to do it, ma'am?"

"I'm afraid not, Josh," I told him as I closed and tied my dress. "My husband was pretty specific, and I have no choice but to do as he said."

I took a step closer to him and stroked my hand firmly up his cock.

"But I'm more than happy to have you watch."

Josh gulped, then jumped away from me as a tall, broad shouldered black man in a dark Canali suit walked past us and into the men's restroom. I looked around, and noticed a small alcove at the end of the hall. Walking over to check it out, I saw a small, doorless room with several plush leather arm chairs and low tables.

"Customers use this area when they need to take longer phone calls, or just want some privacy," Josh said as he came up behind me. It was perfect.

The attractive black man had just come out of the men's room, and I walked up to him with a smile. He smiled back readily, his eyes dipping to my cleavage for a moment before he started to brush past me. I stopped him with a hand on his hard bicep.

"Sir, do you have a minute to lend me a hand?" I asked with a flirty smile. My heart was racing. I knew I was going to go through with it -- I had no choice -- but I still didn't know exactly how to ask for what I needed.

"Anything for a pretty lady," he replied in a deep, sexy voice that made my pussy wet.

Taking him by the hand, I pulled him into the private alcove where Josh was waiting. I was just going to have to tell this stranger exactly what I needed, and hope he was intrigued enough to help me.

Without letting go of his large, warm hand, I opened my other one to reveal the shiny sex toy. His eyebrows shot up in surprise, and I could tell that he knew what it was for. Glancing between the plug and my eyes a few times, he started circling a finger on the palm of my hand.

"Exactly what kind of help did you have in mind?" he asked quietly, with a glance over my shoulder at the Josh.

"I need-- I need you to get this in me," I took a deep breath. "And I need you to let the busboy watch."

Laughing in disbelief, the gorgeous man tried to pull his hand away and looked over his shoulder.

"Is this a joke?" he asked with a smile. "Because girl, you are freaky."

I clung to his hand and stepped closer to him. I had to tip my head back to look up at him, and he smelled amazing. Lifting his hand up to my chest, I covered one of my breasts with his large palm and pressed against him.

"I know," I smiled. "Will you help?"

Kneading my breast with his large hand, he reached around and slid the other one up the back of my thigh and under my dress. When he found nothing but my naked skin underneath, he sucked in a breath and squeezed my bare cheek tightly.

"I did not expect *this*, but hey, I'm not one to look a gift horse in the mouth."

Without letting go of me, he backed me farther into the alcove until the back of my legs bumped into one of the leather chairs. Spinning me around, he put a hand between my shoulder blades and pushed me over. I braced my hands on the plush, leather armrests and arched my back.

"Boy, you'd better make sure no one comes back here," he ordered Josh without looking away from my waiting ass.

The stranger pushed my dress up to my waist and whistled softly. He ran his warm hands up my hips and over my curvy bottom, then pulled my cheeks apart so he could see his target.

"You have got a sweet little backside, but damn, it looks like someone did a number on you," he said, breathing heavily.

I knew that there were fading bruises from the spankings I'd received over the last few days, and the leather belt that Mr. Davis had whipped me with that morning had probably left a few welts.

"Yes, sir," I replied breathlessly. "And if I don't manage to talk you into inserting my plug, I'll be punished again."

He groaned, and ran a thick finger down my crack. After a brief hesitation, he continued under me and slid that it through my wet slit.

"You've got to talk me into it, huh?" he asked with a little laugh. "And just how are you supposed to convince me to accept this difficult assignment?"

"I'll do whatever it takes, sir," I answered breath-lessly, looking back at him over my shoulder.

He met my eyes for a moment, then went back to watching himself stroke me. Mesmerized by the unexpected treat, he continued to fondle me in silence. It was starting to drive me crazy, and I

pushed my pussy against his hand in supplication.
The large man stole a glance at his watch and grimaced.

"I wish I had more time to enjoy *this*," he muttered as he drove a finger into me. "But I've got a table full of clients waiting on me. *Damn.* Give me that toy, girl."

His finger was well lubed with my own juices, and he pressed it against my puckering hole, then slowly forced it inside. It was sharply painful for a moment, and then settled into an uncomfortable ache. He worked it deep into me and thrust in and out a few times while I relaxed around the sensation.

"You have got a *tight* hole here, baby," he laughed. "Not used to taking it in the backdoor?"

"No, sir," I managed. It was starting to feel *good.*

Now that I was relaxing, he put another finger inside me, and *ow!* But oooohhhh. I moaned. I could feel his huge cock rubbing against my hip through his pants and desperately hoped that I'd get some of that, too, before he left me.

He replaced one of his fingers with the tip of the plug, and then eased his other finger fully out as he pushed the toy into my ass. It was a cold stretch, and I whimpered softly as he worked it in, but of course I had no choice but to take it. When he finally had it fully inserted, my little hole closed tightly around the base and locked it into me.

"Now let's talk about that convincing you need to do, girl."

His deep voice sent erotic shivers all the way through me. And so did the sound of his zipper going down. I panted eagerly as I spread my legs apart. I heard the sound of a second zipper, and looked back to see Josh standing in the doorway, stroking his own cock as he stared greedily at my wet pussy.

The gorgeous black man must have had a 10" cock, and it was so thick that my cunt ached as he pushed it in. He entered me slowly. He had to. Although I wanted it, I didn't know if I could take it all. He was *huge*.

"Fuucccccckkkkkkk," he groaned. "That little toy is taking up some space in here, baby. You are so fucking tight!"

His rock hard cock rubbed slowly over my g spot in a long, smooth, slide that had my toes curling. He pulled back slowly, then did it again. Fuck slow.

"Please," I gasped. *"Please!"*

I could hear a wet, slapping sound behind me as the busboy jerked his cock in a desperate rhythm. I wanted this huge black man to fuck me just as hard, just as fast.

With a hoarse grunt, he did.

Pulling himself almost all the way out, he slammed forward so hard that his balls swung up and slapped me. And then he did it again. And again. And--

Oh my God. Getting fucked with the plug clenched tightly in my ass, by a cock bigger than any I'd ever taken, was going to make me come in seconds. And the best part, I thought as my orgasm ripped through me, was that it was all at my husband's command.

"*Fuuccccckkkkkkk!*" he hissed as my pussy pulsed around him. With two more hard thrusts he pulled out and shot hot streams of cum all over the leather chair.

"Unnnngggh!" I heard from Josh as he shot his own load.

The well hung man smoothed my dress back down over the sparkling blue jewel and helped me up. Turning me around to face him, he tipped my chin up and dropped a light kiss on the end of my nose.

"Happy to help, little freak," he said with a wink.

"I'm, uh, going to need a few minutes to clean all this up," the busboy muttered as the big man walked past him. "And then, um, then I guess we can go let your husband know you did it."

"Thank you, Josh," I sighed happily.

I sat in one of the chairs that wasn't covered in cum while he pulled out a white towel and went to work.

Glancing at the clock, I saw that my hour was almost up. I guess I missed out on lunch.

BETHANY'S SUBMISSION - PART 5

A DOMESTIC DISCIPLINE SPANKING ROMANCE

CHAPTER ONE

S itting in the cab with my new anal plug inserted was making me squirm. I can't say it was uncomfortable, but it definitely kept my attention on an area of my body that I normally don't give much thought to.

I was on my way back to the hotel that I was staying at with my husband, Richard. We had flown in for the board meeting he was required to attend today, and I had just left a lunch with him and the CEO. The two men were headed back to the headquarters of the Cummington Group for the remainder of the afternoon, but Richard had given me explicit instructions that he trusted me to follow exactly.

Before this trip, I would have struggled with following his orders for an entire free afternoon in a new city. We both know I would have loved shopping or seeing a show, but this time, that sort of thing wasn't the point of this trip.

I had agreed to use our time away as a sort of Boot Camp to conquer once and for all my resistance to his authority. Richard and I had agreed to base our marriage on a Domestic Discipline lifestyle, but I had always held back in small ways from truly obeying him.

My current submissiveness training had put an end to that.

I smiled in contentment as I realized how far I'd come in such a short time. Agreeing to give him absolute domination over my mind, body, and spirit during this trip had been the best thing I'd ever done for our marriage. Thinking back to all the times I'd resented his control over our lives, I was embarrassed at what I had put both of us through.

It was only when I agreed to let go and trust him, to allow him to use me without argument or hesitation, and to follow his orders without question, that I became truly free. We would be returning home soon, but I shied away from thinking about that.

My submission training wasn't intended as a long term lifestyle, but rather an intense immersion into what true submission meant. We both hoped that it would allow me fully embrace my role as Richard's submissive wife when we returned to our daily lives, and I could only hope that he would be willing to continue requiring my absolute obedience.

Arriving at the hotel, I tipped the cabdriver and headed to the concierge to carry out my husband's orders.

"May I help you, Ma'am?" he asked as I approached the desk.

"Yes, sir," I answered with a smile. "I'm going to need the service of a bellboy."

"Of course, Ma'am," he answered promptly. Discreetly signaling toward the young, uniformed men waiting near the luggage cards, he glanced at the empty floor behind me. "Is your luggage still waiting in the cab?"

"No, we're already checked in. I actually need a different form of discreet assistance up in our room."

I slipped him a $100 bill as I said the word "discreet" which effectively ended his curiosity. Giving me his most professional smile, he politely introduced me to the bellboy, Eddie, and gave him instructions to see to my needs.

As we rode up to my hotel room, I idly wondered whether the baby faced bellboy would balk at my request. Eddie looked about 20 years old and had a sweet eagerness that probably earned him a lot of tips. I caught him stealing a glance at the cleavage on display in my low-cut dress, and he blushed to the tips of his ears.

He was courteous and respectful, and if I'd had a choice in the matter, definitely not the person I would have picked to carry out my husband's instructions. He just didn't seem the type. But of course that's the beauty of obedience. It wasn't up to me, and therefore I didn't hesitate or spend any time worrying about whether I would shock him.

"Do you need me to wait while you pack your bags, Ma'am?" he asked hesitantly as he followed me into our tidy hotel room.

"No, we won't be checking out until later tonight. I need you to help me with something else, and I need to trust that it won't leave this room."

I slipped him another $100 bill and saw his eyes widen as he pocketed it. He swallowed nervously, and I wondered what he imagined I would ask of him.

"Y-yes, Ma'am."

I left him standing near the door and walked over to the thermostat. Knowing how hot I would be over the next few hours, I turned the air conditioning on full blast, then walked to the closet and pulled out my husband's small travel bag. Although I had done the packing for the both of us before we left, Richard had obviously added some things I hadn't been aware of. Just as he'd instructed, I found several rolls of saran wrap and the other goodies he'd left for me.

"What, um, exactly do you need me to do, Ma'am?"

Eddie was craning his neck to try to see what I was doing, and I smiled wickedly before turning to face him. My husband had chosen a short, wrap around dress for me today and instructed me to wear it without bra or panties. It closed with a single tie around my waist, and as I turned back to face the bellboy I pulled it open with one tug and shrugged it off.

As he gaped at my naked body, I wonder if he'd seen the blue jewel glinting from between my cheeks before I'd turned. The protruding end of the anal plug was slightly rounded and held my ass open just enough that the decoration was clearly visible from behind.

At the moment, though, Eddie clearly wasn't wondering about anything but what was right in front of him. His eyes roamed hungrily over my firm, high breasts and smoothly shaven pussy, and I watched with enjoyment as his cock started to swell under his stiff uniform pants.

"M-Ma-Ma'am," he stuttered stupidly.

Little beads of sweat had popped out on his forehead and he licked his lips as he tried to figure out what to say next. He looked so sweetly nervous that it was tempting to toy with him a little bit, but exposing myself to him was starting to excite me and it made me impatient to have his hands on me.

"Eddie, my husband has asked me to be bound and ready for his use when he returns. I need you to help secure and position me properly. Can you do that, please?"

"What? I don't-- I have no idea, um, what you…"

His voice drifted off into silence as he continued to stare at my tits. Having mercy on the boy, I walked up to him and took his hand. It was hot and sweaty, and tightened convulsively around mine as I led him to the bed.

"What *is* that?"

Glancing over my shoulder, I saw his eyes glued to my ass. His finger was hovering over the jeweled end of my anal plug and I watched as he valiantly restrained himself from actually touching me.

"It's something to hold me open for my husband," I answered.

The bellboy turned as red as a beet. I watched in amusement as he pictured what I meant, making his tented pants jerked with excitement. Just to tease him, I pushed my bare bottom toward him, closing the distance to his trembling finger. He groaned and spread his hand open over my firm curves, and then pulled it back as if burned.

"Would your husband, um, approve of me being here?" he asked uneasily.

I turned to face him. He was so close that his protruding cock rubbed against my hip as I pivoted. I swayed slightly from side to side as I answered him, making sure that my stomach stroked his tip, right over the small wet spot growing on the front of his pants.

"Absolutely. He gave me strict instructions on what he needs me to do. He knows that the staff here prides itself on service, and he trusts me to get the help I need from someone who can... handle it."

The boy was literally trembling, and I wondered what he would do once he had me at his mercy. With the A/C blowing, the room had started to cool down and my nipples had hardened into puckered little pebbles. Their tightness wasn't just from the cold, though. My pussy tingled in anticipation, and I certainly hoped that he would take full advantage of the situation once it was out of my hands.

"I need you to wrap me up so that I can wait for my husband's return," I told Eddie as I handed him the rolls of saran wrap.

He looked at me uncertainly, but when he saw I was serious he cautiously unrolled the thin, clear material and did as I asked. I folded my arms behind my back, holding onto my own elbows so that my breasts were thrust forward, and had him bind me the way Richard had instructed.

He started just under my collar bone and tightly wrapped my shoulders and upper chest with the first roll. It effectively pinned my upper arms against my body, and forced Eddie to wrap his arms around me again and again as he circled me with the clear wrap. He was blushing and trembling as his body continuously rubbed against my full breasts, and I didn't try to hide my own excitement as the contact aroused me more and more.

Richard wanted my breasts fully exposed, so once he was done with the top I had him start directly under my lush C cups. He covered my midsection to the top of my hips, binding my crossed arms tightly to my back and ensuring that I was completely at his mercy.

As instructed, I told Eddie to bend my flexible dancers legs at the knees so that my heels rested just under the curve of my ass. He wrapped each leg separately, so that later my husband could move and position me easily while having full access to all entry points. Once the bellboy had completed his task, I looked like an erotic, mummified sex toy. My breasts, cunt, and ass were fully exposed, but I couldn't move myself at all and lay helplessly on the bed before him.

The saran wrap trapped all my body heat, and the contrast between my hot, wrapped skin and the frigid air on my exposed flesh was almost as stimulating as watching Eddie's rising excitement. I could see the moment that the bellboy went from nervous and uncertain to the realization that I was completely docile and restrained.

"Now what?" he asked as he devoured me with his eyes.

"My orders are to have you leave me wrapped and blindfolded," I told him with a smile. "My husband will be back sometime this evening."

"What happens then?" he asked as his pupils dilated. He was compulsively rubbing his palms against the sides of his pants, and I knew if he'd been a little less inhibited he would be actively stroking his rock hard cock.

"That's up to my husband," I answered. "As you can see, my only choice is to accept whatever... he... wants to do to me."

"He must really have a lot of faith in our hotel staff, to have someone he doesn't even know, uh, prepare you like this," Eddie gulped. "I mean, how does he know that you wouldn't get someone who decides to, uh, take advantage of the situation?"

My pussy clenched at his words, which sent a shot of tingling pleasure through my lower regions as it forced me to tighten around my anal plug as well. Complete submission meant that I also surrendered all inhibitions. Being completely at someone else's mercy allowed me to anticipate and enjoy without guilt, and I really, really hoped that the baby faced bellboy would give in and have his way with me.

"And just how would *you* 'take advantage' of this situation, Eddie?" I asked provocatively.

Dragging his eyes off of my outthrust breasts, he looked at me carefully before answering. I wasn't going to give him verbal permission, but I certainly couldn't stop him if he decided to take what he so obviously wanted. Whatever he saw in my eyes gave him his answer, and he carefully set down the unused saran wrap he'd been holding and unzipped his pants.

"I would get some relief for this," he told me in a husky voice as he moved toward the bed.

While the bellboy was wrapping me, he'd gently lowered me down on my back in order to finish my legs. I'd ended up with my head near the middle of the bed and my bent knees on the edge closest to him. Whatever he had in mind required something different, and he grabbed my bound body and rotated me so that my head was hanging off the foot of the bed right in front of him.

This position gave me a perfect view of his hard cock as he leaned over me. It was long and slender. A bluish vein throbbed along its length and the head glistened with precum. His balls were high and tight, and they pressed into my forehead as he reached for my breasts.

"Oh my God," he whispered.

He stroked them gently at first, and then suddenly squeezed so tightly that I gasped. His rough palms stimulated my sensitive nipples, and even as he separated and squeezed my lush globes tight enough to hurt, the friction on my nipples made me moan with excitement.

His cock was bouncing against my face, and I rubbed my cheek against the silken hardness like a cat. Eddie seemed mesmerized by his free access to my breasts, but I wondered how long they would hold his attention with his straining erection so close to my wet mouth. Reaching with my tongue, I managed to lick a few inches as he moved above me. Eddie froze at the moist contact, and then moved back enough that he could line his cock up with my lips.

"You *want* to suck me, don't you," he panted.

He held the base of his shaft and guided it into my open mouth. With my head extended backward he had a straight shot all the way down my throat, and with a low groan he slowly slipped his whole length in. When I felt his balls press into my nose, I shifted my head to the side so I could breathe, and started swallowing to milk his cock with my throat.

"Oh *fuck!*" he gasped.

I felt him swell inside my mouth, so I started to hum to help him along. The vibration was too much for him. Holding my head tightly, he frantically started to fuck my face, thrusting his cock in to the hilt with each stroke. After the strain of his long arousal, it only took a few moments before he came. With another "*fuck!*" he slammed into my face.

His balls completely blocked my nose and I struggled to breathe as he shot spurt after spurt of salty cum deep into my throat. I swallowed as fast as I could, and then jerked my head to the side to try to get some air. Pulling himself out, he was oblivious to the fact that he'd nearly suffocated me, and sank down to his knees next to the bed.

"That was un-fucking-believable," he finally managed. "Do you and your husband play weird games like this all the time? I saw that thing you've got in your ass. You two are into some kinky shit."

Finally somewhat recovered, he started to stand up and tuck himself into his pants. Suddenly realizing that having my head hang upside down probably wasn't very comfortable, he gave me an apologetic look and pushed me up on the bed.

"Is this okay, if I just leave you like this? This is really what you want?" he asked sweetly.

"Actually, you'll need to remember to blindfold me," I reminded him with a nod toward the closet. "And if you don't mind, I'd rather have a pillow under my head."

Eddie grabbed one of my husband's silk ties and wrapped it around head, covering my eyes. Once he'd tied it tightly, he climbed up on the bed next to me so that he could reposition me with my head facing the other direction. He settled a pillow under my head and lightly stroked a hand down my body.

"You are so fucking hot," he whispered.

I arched into his hand. With my vision cut off, every other sense was suddenly hyper aware. I was still completely aroused, and knowing that he was kneeling above me, looking, made me squirm with need.

"Can you see?" he asked in a low voice.

"No."

I heard his zipper go down again, and caught my breath. I had felt vulnerable as soon as he'd bound me, but being blind and powerless took it to a whole new level.

"Eddie," I blurted out. "What are you doing?"

Instead of answering me, I felt the bed shift as he moved on top of me. He straddled my stomach and pushed my breasts together roughly. I could feel his cock, completely hard again, pressing against the plastic encasing me. Even though my breasts were exposed, the wrap was making me slick with sweat, and they were slippery under his hands. He forced them together and then, with a jerk of his hips, he thrust his cock into the tight cleavage he'd made between them.

He was fucking my tits, kneading and pressing them painfully to keep them tight around his long cock. My panting breaths only drove his shaft through the slit he'd made for himself all the faster, and the hot head slid up onto my neck with each thrust.

I had never been used this way, and on top of everything else it made me so horny that my pussy actually hurt. I was going to have to wait, though. Eddie was completely focused on what he was doing, and when he finally came, he rammed into me so hard that his cock hit the base of my chin. Hot cum spurted over my face and lips, and I licked at it greedily, wanting more.

Without a word, I felt him climb off the bed and then heard the sound of water running in the bathroom. I assumed he was cleaning himself up, and wondered if he would come back and wash his cum off my face or leave it there for my husband to find. Either way, I had no choice in the matter.

Blindfolded and bound, I relaxed on the bed to wait for whatever happened was going to happen next.

BETHANY'S SUBMISSION - PART 6

A DOMESTIC DISCIPLINE SPANKING ROMANCE

CHAPTER ONE

I didn't know how long I'd been laying on the bed in our hotel room, blindfolded, bound, and used. The bellboy who had helped me prepare myself for my husband had washed his cum off of my face and chest before leaving, but there had been no way for me to tell how much time was passing other than the growing stiffness in my bent legs and arms.

I surprised myself by easily ignoring that discomfort, though. I relaxed on the bed, content to wait for my husband, Richard, to return. The submissiveness training he'd given me over the last few days had been a complete success. I was perfectly content with my situation — not because it was enjoyable, because it wasn't, really — but because I'd surrendered my will to him completely, and this is what he wanted of me.

It was utterly freeing, and as my body waited, my heart soared, filled with love and appreciation that Richard had been willing to do this for me. The only sour note was the knowledge that this business trip — and the Boot Camp style training we'd agreed to — were about to come to an end.

I knew that I'd have no trouble submitting to him when we returned home... as long as he continued to dominate me. My only fear was that he would slack off. If he gave me room to return to my former ways — the subtle resistance to his authority that he'd put up with for far too long — I couldn't be entirely sure that I wouldn't start to slide back into old habits.

I bit my lip, trying to picture going back to the version of our relationship we'd had before. It hadn't been bad, exactly, but this was so much better. I'd discovered the utter freedom of letting my husband own me completely, and now I craved it like a drug.

Finally, I heard the lock click on the hotel room door. My heart started to race, and I hoped that I could convince Richard that what had started as training could become the next evolution of our Domestic Discipline lifestyle.

I heard footsteps approach the bed — just one set. Was it my husband, or had he sent someone else to use me? I instinctively tipped my head toward the sound, even though I couldn't see a thing. I never would have imagined that Richard would let other men have their way with me, but I understood that it was part of my training. A way to guarantee that I didn't balk at anything he required of me.

And the truth was, knowing that he'd ordered it, I'd allowed myself to enjoy it.

This time, though, I secretly hoped that my final test would come from the man I'd married. I'd vowed to love, honor, and obey him, and I was suddenly desperate to have the chance to show him how completely I could honor that vow.

I wanted him to know that he could ask anything of me, use me in any way that he chose, and that I would willingly — *eagerly* — comply.

The footsteps stopped near the bed. Whoever it was, I wondered if he liked what he saw.

Following my husband's directions, I'd asked the bellboy to wrap my body tightly in saran wrap, binding me to await Richard's pleasure. My arms were folded behind my back, a position that thrust my lush breasts forward and forced my back to arch a bit, all the better to display them.

Eddie, the bellboy, had left them uncovered and then taken advantage of the situation by fucking them before he'd left me. He'd also bound each of my legs separately, bent up at the knee so that my heels rested just under the curve of my ass, leaving full access to my cunt and my ass — currently plugged with a blue-jeweled sex toy.

"Bethany," Richard's voice washed over me, making me tremble with excitement. "I'm so proud of you."

"Thank you, sir," I answered proudly. I could hear the sincerity in his voice, and it made me glow with pleasure.

"Our flight leaves in a few hours," he told me. "You'll need to pack for us, which doesn't leave a lot of time for training. Are you ready to submit to me, Bethany?"

"Yes, sir," I replied eagerly. "Always."

"I can see that you followed my directions. Tell me what happened when you came back to the hotel."

I told him every detail. I had no qualms about describing how Eddie had gotten turned on by my naked submissiveness, or how he had fucked my mouth, and then my tits. I knew that I couldn't hold anything back from my husband, and that even if my behavior earned a punishment I would also be proving my obedience by readily admitting how I'd submitted to the other man's use of me.

"You did well," he said, confirming what I'd expected. "But you know I'll have to punish you."

"Yes, sir."

"Do you want me to remove your blindfold, Bethany?"

I licked my lips, considering. If he did, I'd be able to see what was coming. The anticipation of a blow could be worse than the actual sting. But would it be worse to have it fall with no warning whatsoever?

"Bethany…" Richard prompted me. My hesitation in answering clearly irritated him, and as soon as I realized that, I knew there was only one answer I could give: "I want whatever you choose, sir. I'm grateful for whatever you decide."

"Good girl," he said approvingly. I swear I could hear the smile in his voice, and I flushed with pleasure.

His hand cupped my cheek, and he ran his thumb over my lips lovingly. I gasped, longing to taste him, but he'd already moved on — running his large hand down the front of my body to squeeze my breasts.

My nipples were pebbled with excitement, and he pinched them lightly, and then made me cry out as he twisted them sharply. The pain shot through me, straight down to my already-damp pussy. As the pain faded, a warm tingle of arousal replaced it, and I started to pant with excitement.

Was this my punishment? Or had he found a new way to reward me?

"You've earned a spanking, Bethany."

I could hear the excitement in his voice, and I started to twist on the bed, anxious to roll over and please him.

"No," he said, stopping me with a firm hand on my hip. "Spread your legs."

I settled onto my back, immediately opening for him. My shaved pussy was pink and wet, and I spread my legs wide enough that he'd be able to see just how happy obeying him made me. I wasn't trying to get out of my punishment, but I also hoped the sight would inspire him to fuck me afterward.

I really, really wanted him to fuck me.

Smack!

"Ahhhh!" I screamed. I couldn't help it. He'd slapped my cunt. My knees jerked up involuntarily and the hot sting was immediately followed by a tingling warmth that felt much too good to be considered punishment. "Oh, Richard," I moaned.

"Be still, Bethany," he ordered in a husky voice.

I felt the bed shift as he sat down next to me, holding me down with one arm while he started rhythmically slapping my pussy with the other. His spanking got harder and harder, until I was writhing under his hand, completely incapable of doing as I was told.

I couldn't hold still.

"Oh, God! Richard! Please!"

Every slap made me tighten up inside, squeezing against the butt plug I'd worn all day and sending sharp zing of excitement to my clit. I knew one more would send me over the edge.

But I didn't get it.

The bed shifted again, and Richard moved away from me. I had to bite my lip to keep from begging for more, but I knew that I wasn't allowed. He'd give me what he wanted to give me, and only when he was ready.

I heard the rustle of clothing being removed, and I moaned in excitement. Then Richard's hands were back on me, stroking between my legs too lightly to do anything other than frustrate me — but as soon as I had the thought I relaxed.

It was his right to frustrate me if he wanted to.

He pushed his fingers inside me, wetting them, while his other hand stroked the jeweled butt plug he'd ordered me to have a stranger insert earlier in the day. He slid it out slowly, making my anus clench at the loss. It had definitely stretched me open, and he immediately replaced it with the fingers he'd made slick from my juices.

"I'm going to fuck your ass, Bethany," he told me.

"Yes, sir," I answered dutifully, whimpering a little as he added another finger and forced my body to open wider for him. Not being able to see made me focus all my attention on the sensation of his fingers inside my virgin channel, and I sucked in a breath as he worked to loosen me up. It stung, sharp little bursts of pain that ramped up my excitement and gave me an unfamiliar sense of fullness that I couldn't tell if I liked or not.

Not that it mattered. My body was his to use as he would.

Richard's breathing was coming faster and faster, and he pulled his fingers out abruptly and knelt between my legs, pushing my bent knees up to my shoulders. I felt the wide head of his cock slide down my slick, pink slit, moistening it, and then press against my puckered hole.

"I've wanted to do this for a long time, Bethany."

"Why didn't you?" I gasped the question out without thinking, but as soon as the words left my mouth I knew the answer. I'd been too stubborn and argumentative. I hadn't been the submissive wife my husband deserved. But this trip — my training — had changed everything.

I knew that Richard would never hesitate to take what he wanted from me again.

He drove his cock into me, hilting himself with one thrust. His thick shaft felt like it had torn me open, even after being stretched all day. I could feel tears leaking out of my eyes, wetting the silk of the tie that the bellboy had used to blindfold me. Despite that, my husband's satisfied groan made me smile with pride.

"God, Bethany, you're so tight back here," he praised me, starting to fuck my ass in earnest. His vigorous thrusts made me burn, and I welcomed the proof that I was being used for his pleasure. Richard dug his hands into my hips, adjusting the angle so he could pound into me even harder.

My body had never felt so sore, but despite the pain, the pleasure of submitting to him on top of the excitement from earlier had me close to coming.

"Richard, please sir, may I?" I begged, hoping he'd know what I meant.

"No."

He pulled out abruptly, leaving me gasping with need. Before I had time to wonder what he wanted to do with me, he'd pushed my legs down and pulled me lower on the bed, shoving me beneath his body and straddling my chest.

"I'm going to come in your mouth, Bethany. Open."

I obeyed without thinking, but when he shoved his cock into my face I almost gagged. It was sour. He'd just had it in my ass.

He didn't give me any time to to think about it, though. He gripped the back of my hair, fisting his hand in my hair, and yanked my head backward. He rose up on his knees and bent over my face, driving himself deep into my throat.

"Suck, Bethany," he gritted out, demanding that I do more than just lay there and take it.

I swirled my tongue around his throbbing shaft, slurping in the residue of my anal initiation and using my cheeks to do as he'd ordered. His cock started to swell, filling my throat until I couldn't get any air except the little bit I managed to pull in through my nose.

I arched up under him, my whole existence shrinking to my husband's dirty cock down my throat. I sucked and swallowed, determined to give him what he deserved and earn the reward of his hot seed down my throat. He pulled my head back farther, pounding into me in a finally frenzy.

"Beeeeeeee," he groaned, slipping into his pet name for me as he finally shot his load, pumping streams of hot, salty cum deep inside me.

I swallowed desperately, determined to savor every drop. When he finally pulled out, I licked my lips, cleaning up the both the salty and the sour residue that coated my face.

"Bethany," Richard said tenderly, pulling my blindfold off. You've done very well. I think we can both agree that your training has been a success."

"Yes, sir," I answered, giddy with happiness at his praise.

He left me on the bed while he called down to housekeeping to request scissors. The saran wrap was too tight to remove without them. Richard headed for the shower while we waited. The water was still running in there when a knock came on the door, and after a moment's indecision I called out, "Enter."

Whether the hotel staff would be shocked to find me in this position or not, it wasn't my concern. If this was how my husband chose to leave me, then I had nothing to be ashamed of.

The door opened slowly, and Eddie the bellboy peeked around the corner. When he saw me on the bed, he smiled and walked in more confidently.

"I wondered if you'd still be here." He looked me over, no doubt noticing that my anal plug had been tossed to the side and seeing the dried cum on my face. "Your husband came back?" he asked.

"Yes, he's in the shower. I think he's ready to release me."

"He called down for scissors," Eddie confirmed, holding them out and then, blushing when he realized that of course I couldn't take them, putting them awkwardly on the credenza. "Um, I guess I'll just go—"

"Not yet." Richard stepped out of the bathroom, wearing the plush robe that the hotel had provided. "Are you the young man who assisted my wife earlier?"

"Y-y-yes," Eddie stuttered nervously. "How did you know?"

"I requested that they send you up with the scissors."

Eddie blanched, looking truly frightened. "She, um, said that you wanted... I mean, that it would be okay..." his words trailed off uncertainly as he gulped.

Richard smiled reassuringly. "You've done nothing wrong. We're going to check out shortly, and I wanted a chance to personally thank you."

Eddie relaxed a little, but still looked nervous.

"Sure, um, no problem. Anything I can do to help, uh, sir."

"I'm glad to hear it," Richard answered heartily. "As my wife no doubt told you, she has been in training. She's learned to obey me, but now her training is complete. It's time to test her submissiveness as we return to our everyday lives. Can you help with that, young man?"

Eddie nodded, starting to look excited.

"Great. I need to shave and dress for the flight. Please release her from her bonds, and then punish her for the moment of reluctance she showed earlier when I put my cock in her mouth."

Richard went back into the bathroom, shutting the door behind him without another word. Eddie hesitated for another moment, and then picked up the scissors and walked over to me. Sliding them carefully under the edge of the saran wrap, he started snipping through the tight plastic. Blood rushed back into my arms as he freed me, making them tingle and burn. I gasped at the pins and needles sensation, and his hand jerked in surprise at the sound, nicking my skin.

"Oh no! I'm so sorry," he burst out. A drop of blood welled up on my side, next to my breast. He looked around for something to staunch it with, settling on some tissue. He dabbed at the blood, his knuckles rubbing against the side of my breast.

Richard hadn't allowed me to come, and my body instantly responded. I wished Richard had ordered

Eddie to fuck me, but I doubted that letting me come was the "punishment" my husband had had in mind.

Eddie was obviously thinking along the same lines, as his cock rose to attention and he swiped at the blood a little too enthusiastically, managing to feel me up in the process. He glanced at the bathroom door nervously, and finally removed his hand from my breasts.

Reaching for the scissors again, he muttered: "I'll be more careful this time, I promise."

I spread my legs for him, giving him the chance to slip the sharp shears against my skin and release them. Once I was free, he helped me up from the bed, looking uncertain about what to do next.

"What did your husband mean, punish you?" he asked after a moment, licking his lips.

"I don't know," I answered honestly. "He usually spanks me." I pointed to the wooden paddle that Richard had brought from home.

"Okay," Eddie agreed, starting to look excited. "Um, I guess you should bend over."

"Do you want me on your lap?" I asked, guessing that he'd enjoy it much more from that position.

He nodded jerkily, grabbing the paddle and sitting on the edge of the bed. I laid myself out across his legs, rubbing against his straining erection.

Crack!

Eddie brought the paddle down on my well-used ass, hard. I flinched, sliding across his lap with the force of the blow. "Nnnggghhh," he moaned, thrusting up against me.

He brought the paddle down again on my other cheek, making it burn and thrusting against me again. He didn't give me any warm up, just cracked the paddle down again and again, until tears were streaming down my face and his cock was stabbing into my stomach with desperate urgency.

I lost count of the strokes, and just gave in to the fiery pain. I knew he wouldn't stop until he came. Finally, he dropped the paddle and grabbed me, grinding up against me as the warm heat of his cum pooled in his lap between us.

"Nicely done," Richard said. I relaxed on Eddie's lap, sure by his immediate tension that the bellboy hadn't known my husband was watching.

My lower body was on fire from the harsh paddling, and my stomach was sticky with the boy's cum. Richard helped me up and told me to go clean myself up. Eddie looked mortified, but Richard didn't comment on the mess in his lap. He just slipped him a bill and hustled him out the door, then joined me in the bathroom.

"Bethany, I'm going to go grab a drink in the bar," he told me. "Pack our things and be downstairs in an hour. We have a flight to catch."

"Yes, sir," I answered obediently, ducking my head as I worried my lip with my teeth. I wanted to ask him what was in store for us at home, and whether he'd continue to treat me the way I'd come to crave on this trip, but I didn't want to be too forward.

As if he read my mind, Richard stepped closer and gently tipped my chin up. Kissing me tenderly, he told me what I wanted to hear. "Even though your Boot Camp is over, BeeBee, I want you to stay obedient."

"I will, Richard, I promise!"

"Can you continue to submit to my authority in all things? Obey me without question?"

"Yes, sir. Always."

"Good girl. Don't come yet," he grinned, nodding toward the shower. "I want to save that for later."

"When?" I asked breathlessly.

"Remember the plane ride here?" I nodded, flashing back to my shock when he'd had our seat mate fuck me with a dildo… and then fuck me for real in the cramped airplane bathroom. "This time, I've made sure we won't have anyone sitting with us," he told me. "I'll give you your reward once you're in the air," he promised before leaving.

I smiled happily. I couldn't wait.

Be the first to find out about all of Lee Riley's new releases, book sales, and freebies by joining her VIP Mailing List. Join today and get a FREE book -- instantly!

Check Lee Riley's website spicybestsellers.com for more books.

GET A FREE BOOK!

Be the first to find out about all of Lee Riley's new releases, book sales, and freebies by joining her VIP Mailing List. Join today and get a FREE book -- instantly!

Check Lee Riley's website spicybestsellers.com for more books.

Ingram Content Group UK Ltd.
Milton Keynes UK
UKHW021005130623
423366UK00014B/356

9 781088 115893